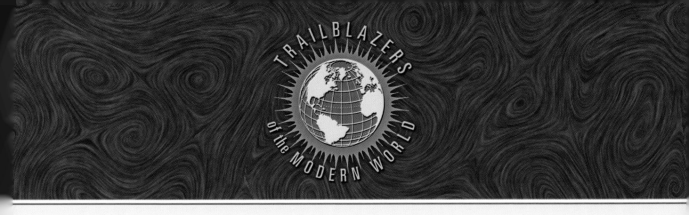

THEODORE ROOSEVELT

By Geoffrey M. Horn

WORLD ALMANAC® LIBRARY

Please visit our web site at: www.worldalmaclibrary.com
For a free color catalog describing World Almanac® Library's list
of high-quality books and multimedia programs, call 1-800-848-2928 (USA)
or 1-800-387-3178 (Canada). World Almanac® Library's fax: (414) 332-3567.

Library of Congress Cataloging-in-Publication Data

Horn, Geoffrey M.
    Theodore Roosevelt / by Geoffrey M. Horn.
      p. cm. — (Trailblazers of the modern world)
    Includes bibliographical references and index.
    Summary: Biography of the twenty-sixth president of the United States, discussing his personal life,
education, and political career.
    ISBN 0-8368-5092-0 (lib. bdg.)
    ISBN 0-8368-5252-4 (softcover)
    1. Roosevelt, Theodore, 1858-1919—Juvenile literature. 2. Presidents—United States—Biography—
Juvenile literature. [1. Roosevelt, Theodore, 1858-1919. 2. Presidents.] I. Title. II. Series.
E757.H84   2003
973.91'1—dc21
[B]   2003042296

First published in 2004 by
World Almanac® Library
330 West Olive Street, Suite 100
Milwaukee, WI 53212 USA

Copyright © 2004 by World Almanac® Library.

Project manager: Jonny Brown
Editor: Jim Mezzanotte
Design and page production: Scott M. Krall
Photo research: Diane Laska-Swanke
Indexer: Walter Kronenberg

Printed in the United States of America

1 2 3 4 5 6 7 8 9 07 06 05 04 03

TABLE of CONTENTS

Words that appear in the glossary are printed in **boldface**
type the first time they occur in the text.

CHAPTER 1

AMERICAN HERO

Heroes come in many forms. When some people think of a hero, they picture a warrior who risks death to win fame and glory on the battlefield. Others define a hero as a powerful leader who works to improve people's lives. Heroes can be explorers who go to enormous lengths to learn about the world. A hero can also be anyone, famous or not, who overcomes huge obstacles in order to lead a productive life.

By all these measures, Theodore Roosevelt—often known as Teddy Roosevelt, or by his initials, TR—was one of the greatest heroes of his day. He was a man of tremendous intelligence, energy, and ambition. Although he was far from perfect, most historians today rank him among the ten best presidents in the history of the United States.

OVERCOMING OBSTACLES

Born in 1858, Roosevelt had to overcome many obstacles in order to become a success. He was a sickly boy with poor eyesight, and he often had terrible attacks of asthma. When he was twenty-five years old, his wife and mother died on the same day. TR was devastated by the loss, but he did not let it destroy him. Instead, he left his home in New York and went out West, where he rebuilt his life as a rancher and cowboy.

With his city manners, spectacles, thin frame, and high-pitched voice, he sometimes had a difficult time getting the frontiersmen to take him seriously. TR believed that the best way to prove his manhood was

A Face on Mount Rushmore

Each year, more than 2.5 million people travel to the Black Hills of South Dakota to visit one of the world's most remarkable monuments—Mount Rushmore. Carved into a mountainside are the faces of four U.S. presidents: George Washington, Thomas Jefferson, Abraham Lincoln, and Theodore Roosevelt.

In choosing these four presidents, the monument's creator, Gutzon Borglum, honored four men who helped establish, preserve, and expand the nation. TR had been chosen, Borglum said, because by starting the construction of the Panama Canal he had "joined the waters of the great East and West seas"—the Atlantic and Pacific Oceans.

Using dynamite blasts, jackhammers, drills, and other tools, Borglum's work crew took fourteen years to carve the four faces on Mount Rushmore. TR's head was the last to be finished, in 1941—the same year Borglum died. Like those of the other presidents, TR's face is about 60 feet (18 meters) high, about as tall as a six-story building.

Theodore Roosevelt (second from right) is one of four U.S. presidents honored at Mount Rushmore. The other three (from left) are George Washington, Thomas Jefferson, and Abraham Lincoln.

In this illustration by W.G. Read, TR leads his "Rough Riders" to victory in Cuba during the Spanish-American War. His success in the war made him a military hero.

This 1903 photo shows President Roosevelt addressing a crowd in Evanston, Illinois. TR used the presidency as a "bully pulpit" to rally public support for his policies and programs.

through hard physical work and, if possible, by showing his courage in battle. In 1898, when the United States went to war with Spain, he got his chance. TR gave up his desk job in Washington, D.C., and joined the U.S. Army. As the leader of the 1st Volunteer **Cavalry Regiment**—known as the "Rough Riders"—he fought against Spanish troops in Cuba. He showed tremendous bravery and leadership, and when he came home to the United States, he was hailed as a military hero.

TR'S ACHIEVEMENTS

Roosevelt entered politics at a time when state and local governments were very corrupt. Political positions were often bought and sold, and many politicians took bribes. TR took a stand against this corruption. He worked hard to reform American public life—first as the youngest member of the New York State legislature, then as police commissioner of New York City, later as governor of New York State, and finally as the twenty-sixth president of the United States.

As president, TR was an activist. He spoke his mind and used the presidency as a **bully pulpit** to win public support for measures he favored. TR believed the nation needed to combine economic power with military muscle. To insure that U.S. naval and commerical ships could reach destinations easily, he pushed for the construction of the Panama Canal, which allows vessels to pass between the Atlantic and Pacific Oceans without having to travel around the southern tip of South America. TR was also the first U.S. president to take an active role in preserving the country's forests and wildlife.

Out of office, TR was a tireless writer and explorer. He went on safari in Africa, and he almost died while exploring an unknown region of Brazil. In all, TR wrote about three dozen books on topics ranging from U.S. history to African animals.

Still used by ships today, the Panama Canal is one of TR's lasting legacies.

Presidential "Firsts"

President Theodore Roosevelt was exactly 42 years and 322 days old when he took office, making him the youngest president in U.S. history. In addition to this distinction, Roosevelt was the first American president to:

Win the Nobel Peace Prize

Travel overseas during his term as president

Fly in an airplane

Own a car

Go underwater in a submarine

Have a telephone in his home

Aviation was still a novelty when TR took his first plane ride in 1910. He is in a plane built by the Wright brothers.

If Roosevelt's heroic qualities were easy to recognize, so were his failings. He had a huge ego, and he took himself very seriously. His accomplishments were genuine, but he was not at all bashful about telling the world about them.

Although TR won the Nobel Peace Prize in 1906 for settling a conflict between Russia and Japan, he was not really a man of peace. In a speech to the Naval War College, in 1897, he stated: "All the great masterful

A formal portrait of Roosevelt during his later years. Most historians consider TR to be among the ten best presidents in U.S. history.

races have been fighting races, and the minute that a race loses the hard fighting virtues, then, no matter what else it may retain, no matter how skilled in commerce and finance, in science or art, it has lost its right to stand as the equal of the best." After a century of numerous conflicts in which tens of millions of people lost their lives, many Americans today are not nearly as certain as TR was about the beneficial effects of warfare.

Like some later U.S. presidents, TR believed the United States could be powerful enough to go it alone in foreign affairs. He backed the takeover of Hawaii and the Philippines in 1898 because he favored the expansion of U.S. power in the Pacific. This strategy helped make the United States a global giant. It came at a steep price, however, because it set the United States on a collision course with Japan and other Asian nations.

The Man in the Arena

TR believed in action. He had little respect for people who could only stand on the sidelines, criticizing and complaining. He made his views clear in this speech in Paris, France, in 1910.

It is not the critic who counts; not the man who points out how the strong man stumbles, or where the doer of deeds could have done them better. The credit belongs to the man who is actually in the arena, whose face is marred by dust and sweat and blood; who strives valiantly; who errs, and comes short again and again, because there is no effort without error and shortcoming; but who does actually strive to do the deeds; who knows the great enthusiasms, the great devotions; who spends himself in a worthy cause; who at the best knows in the end the triumph of high achievement, and who at the worst, if he fails, at least fails while daring greatly, so that his place shall never be with those cold and timid souls who know neither victory nor defeat.

CHAPTER 2

"TEEDIE"

One of the earliest known photos of Theodore Roosevelt, taken when he was four years old. As a child, he was called "Teedie."

Theodore Roosevelt was born in New York City on the evening of October 27, 1858. He was called "Teedie" as a boy, to distinguish him from his father, who was also named Theodore. The elder Roosevelt, known as "Thee" or "Greatheart," came from a Dutch merchant family that had been living in New York for two hundred years. He was one of the city's most influential men—wealthy, intelligent, popular, and energetic. TR later said of his father that he was "the best man I ever knew," but also "the only man of whom I was ever really afraid."

Greatheart loved to dance and go horseback riding in Central Park. But although he enjoyed a comfortable lifestyle, he had what he described as a "troublesome conscience"—he was bothered by the suffering of the poor, especially of poor children. He was one of the founders of the Children's Aid Society, which was established in New York City in 1853 to help orphans who were living on the street. He was also a founder of the New York Orthopedic Hospital, a place where children with bone problems could be treated. The Roosevelt family knew about orthopedic medicine because Teedie's older sister Anna ("Bamie") had a bone disease that affected her spine.

Teedie's mother, Martha Bulloch Roosevelt, was born in Connecticut, but she was actually a daughter of the South. Martha, or "Mittie," spent most of her childhood in Roswell, Georgia, where her father owned a mansion called Bulloch Hall. The elder Roosevelt first met Mittie while visiting Bulloch Hall in 1850, and they were married there three years later, in the Bulloch dining room. The mansion, which is now part of the Roswell Historic District, can still be visited today.

Mittie was considered one of the most beautiful and charming women in New York, but her Southern background was very different from that of Greatheart. Her parents had owned slaves, and as a girl she was provided with a personal slave child. Mittie's pro-slavery views set her apart from most Northerners and from some members of her family, especially her husband.

Teedie's mother, "Mittie" (bottom, left), grew up in a Georgia mansion, while his father, "Greatheart" (bottom, right), came from a well-established family in New York City.

TR's Family Tree

Theodore Roosevelt
>   Born: October 27, 1858, in New York City
>
>   Died: January 6, 1919, in Oyster Bay, New York

His mother: Martha ("Mittie") Bulloch Roosevelt
>   Born: July 8, 1834, in Hartford, Connecticut
>
>   Died: February 14, 1884, in New York City

His father: Theodore ("Thee" or "Greatheart") Roosevelt
>   Born: September 22, 1831, in New York City
>
>   Died: February 9, 1878, in New York City

Parents were married: December 22, 1853, in Roswell, Georgia

TR's sisters and brothers: Anna ("Bamie"; 1855–1931);
>   Elliott ("Ellie"; 1860–1894); Corinne ("Conie"; 1861–1933)

TR's first wife: Alice Hathaway Lee Roosevelt
>   Born: July 29, 1861, in Chestnut Hill, Massachusetts
>
>   Married TR: October 27, 1880, in Brookline, Massachusetts
>
>   Children: Alice Lee (1884–1980)
>
>   Died: February 14, 1884, in New York City

TR's second wife: Edith Kermit Carow Roosevelt
>   Born: August 6, 1861, in Norwich, Connecticut
>
>   Married TR: December 2, 1886, in London, England
>
>   Children: Theodore (1887–1944); Kermit (1889–1943);
>   Ethel Carow (1891–1977); Archibald Bulloch
>   ("Archie"; 1894–1979); Quentin (1897–1918)
>
>   Died: September 30, 1948, in Oyster Bay, New York

CIVIL WAR

Beginning in April 1861, when Teedie was not yet three years old, the United States was torn apart by the **Civil War**. For the next four years, forces from the North, or Union, fought against troops from the South, or **Confederacy**. The North and South were divided on many issues, but the central cause of the conflict was a

A funeral procession for President Abraham Lincoln on April 25, 1865, passed right by a house owned by Teedie's grandfather, Cornelius Van Schaack Roosevelt. Some scholars believe the two young children visible in the open window are Teedie and his brother, Elliott.

dispute over slavery. The North wanted to end the enslavement of African-Americans throughout the country, and the South wanted to continue the practice.

The Civil War split the nation, and it also divided the Roosevelt household. Greatheart had lived in the North his whole life, and he sided with the Union. Mittie, meanwhile, took the Confederate side. During the years of the Civil War, Mittie's mother and sister—two more supporters of the Southern cause—spent a great deal of time with the Roosevelts in New York, while two of Mittie's brothers were fighting for the Confederacy.

In 1863, the federal government passed a new law requiring all able-bodied men to serve in the Union army. Any healthy man who did not want to fight would have to pay a fee of three hundred dollars—a very large sum in those days. By this time, Teedie's father was in his early thirties, and he was still healthy and strong. He believed in the Union cause, but to preserve family harmony he paid the three hundred dollars instead of donning a soldier's uniform. Later in life, the younger Roosevelt would come to have deep regret about his father's decision. Some writers have suggested that one reason TR was so anxious to fight in a war was that he wanted to make up for his father's lack of wartime service.

TR and FDR

The United States has had two presidents named Roosevelt. Theodore Roosevelt (TR), the nation's twenty-sixth president, served from 1901 to 1909. Franklin Delano Roosevelt (FDR), the thirty-second U.S. president, held the office from 1933 until his death in 1945. The two men were distant cousins.

Theodore Roosevelt was more closely related to FDR's famous wife, Eleanor Roosevelt. She was TR's niece—the daughter of his younger brother, Elliott. Since Elliott died in 1894, it was TR who "gave away" the bride when Eleanor married Franklin eleven years later.

U.S. president Franklin D. Roosevelt was TR's distant cousin, and his wife, Eleanor, was TR's niece. In this photo, the president and first lady have just left Easter services in 1941.

CHILDHOOD PAINS AND PLEASURES

Teedie was a frail child. His asthma was so severe that his breathing difficulties might last for weeks at a time. "One of my memories," he later wrote, "is of my father walking up and down the room with me in his arms at night when I was a very small person, and of sitting up in bed gasping, with my father and mother trying to help me."

Since modern medicines to treat asthma had not yet been developed, his parents had to make do with home remedies. To open up his congested airways, they would let the young boy drink strong black coffee, make him smoke a cigar, rub him hard on the chest, or give him syrup that would make him throw up. Sometimes his father wrapped him in a blanket and took him on a nighttime ride through the streets of Manhattan, hoping that the fresh air would help him breathe.

Because of his poor health, Teedie spent much of his time indoors, reading. He loved adventure stories—tales he described as "first-class, good healthy stories, interesting in the first place, and in the next place teaching manliness, decency, and good conduct."

When Teedie did go outside, he took an intense interest in the world of nature. He was fascinated by birds, insects, frogs, snakes, and other creatures, and he filled the Roosevelt family home with specimens—alive and dead—for his collection. Teedie loved camping as well as hunting, a sport he pursued avidly after he was given a double-barreled shotgun at the age of fourteen.

Teedie, his brother, and his two sisters were mostly schooled at home. One of their few close friends from outside the household was Edith Kermit Carow. Edith was the same age as Teedie's younger sister, Corinne ("Conie"), but Teedie also became very fond of her. When the Roosevelt family departed in 1869 for a year-long trip to Europe, Teedie wrote in his diary that parting from her was very difficult and that he "cried a great deal" because Edith did not join them on the trip.

The grim-faced young man with beard and bandana is TR at age eighteen. With him are his brother Elliott, his sister Conie (right), and Edith Carow, a family friend. Many years later, Edith would become TR's second wife.

CHAPTER 3

THE DARKEST DAY

In the autumn of 1876, Theodore Roosevelt enrolled at Harvard College in Cambridge, Massachusetts. Despite his uncertain health, he had already seen more of the world than most people his age. In 1869, the Roosevelts had begun a grand tour of Europe. Three years later, they had journeyed to an even more exotic locale—Egypt. After spending the winter cruising along the Nile River, they had traveled to Jerusalem and other Middle East sites, then back to Europe, and finally home to New York. During his months on the Nile, young Teedie developed a passion for shooting birds and then studying and preserving the dead creatures through the art of **taxidermy**.

By the time he entered Harvard College, TR was strong enough to join the rowing team. He also developed his skills at boxing and ice skating.

Another change had also affected Teedie during his teen years. After a particularly severe bout of asthma, the boy had a serious conversation with his father. "Theodore," his father said, "you have the mind but you have not the body, and without the help of the body the mind cannot go as far as it should. You must make your body. It is hard drudgery to make one's body, but I know you will do it."

Teedie began to work out daily, both at a nearby gym and on the exercise equipment his father brought home. His body remained skinny, but his strength and endurance improved, as did his overall health.

During his Harvard years, TR experienced dramatic changes in his personal life. In the autumn of 1877, while TR was in his sophomore year, his father began to experience severe stomach cramps. Greatheart put on a brave face when TR came home for the Christmas holidays. In the following weeks, however, as the cancer inside him grew, his agony became unbearable. On February 9, 1878, TR received an urgent telegram telling him he needed to come home right away. He took the overnight train, but when he arrived in New York he heard the dreadful news: Greatheart was already dead.

This photo of TR's room at Harvard was taken by his sister Bamie.

TR's grief was deep. Recalling how his father had helped him overcome his asthma, he regretted not having been of much use during his father's final illness. He wrote that he was "as much inferior to Father morally and mentally as physically." Long after his death, Greatheart remained an important presence in his son's life. TR's sister Conie said that many years later, "when the college boy of 1878 was entering upon his duties as President of the United States, he told me frequently that he never took any serious step or made any vital decisions for his country without thinking first what position his father would have taken on the question."

EDITH AND ALICE

For most of their young lives, Theodore Roosevelt and Edith Carow had been close friends. Many people who

TR's first wife, Alice Hathaway Lee Roosevelt.

knew them thought that someday they might get married. In the summer of 1878, however, the two teenagers quarreled. A few months after their breakup, TR fell in love with someone else.

TR's new love was Alice Hathaway Lee. She was tall and slim, with honey-blonde curls, a radiant smile, a fondness for tennis, and a personality so enchanting her friends and relatives called her Sunshine. "You see that girl there?" he told a friend. "I am going to marry her. She won't have me, but I am going to have her." She refused his first proposal of marriage in June 1879. By the beginning of 1880, however, the arrangements had been made. Their wedding took place at a Unitarian church in Brookline, Massachusetts, on October 27, 1880, the date of TR's twenty-second birthday. Edith—now nineteen, like Alice—was one of the invited guests.

TR in Love

In this diary entry for February 13, 1880, TR described his passion for Alice.

I do not think ever a man loved a woman more than I love her; for a year and a quarter now I have never (even when hunting) gone to sleep or waked up without thinking of her; and I doubt if an hour has passed that I have not thought of her. And now I can scarcely realize that I can hold her in my arms and kiss her and caress her and love her as much as I choose.

HIGH HOPES

To all outward appearances, TR's life in the early 1880s could hardly have been more happy. When his father died, TR inherited about $125,000. From that sum, plus interest, he could safely draw about $8,000 a year. This amount might not seem like much today, but at the time it was more than the annual salary earned by the president of Harvard.

TR had graduated from Harvard near the top of his class, excelling both in the natural sciences and in his newer interest, political economy. He was married to a woman whom he adored and who loved him in return. His health had improved, and when he entered Columbia Law School in the autumn of 1880 he knew what he wanted to do with his life. He joined the Republican Party and, a year later, ran for a seat in the New York State assembly.

Roosevelt won election to the state assembly in November 1881 by a margin of 3,490 votes to 1,989. Still only twenty-three years of age, he was the youngest

TR on Women's Rights

No issue was more hotly debated while Roosevelt was in college than whether women should have the same rights as men. On this subject, as on many others, TR's views were forward-looking. In his senior year, he wrote:

As regards the laws relating to marriage, there should be the most absolute equality preserved between the two sexes. I do not think the woman should assume the man's name. . . . I would have the word "obey" used not more by the wife than the husband.

TR's first child, Alice Lee Roosevelt.

member of the assembly—and one of the most determined. TR came to Albany, the state capital, at a time when big businesses routinely bribed politicians to buy their support. He became a crusader for clean government, often opposing the leaders of his own party. Soon he was one of the brightest stars in New York State Republican politics.

A CURSE ON THE HOUSE

During the summer of 1883, Roosevelt learned that he was going to become a father. His wife's pregnancy appeared to go well, although Alice, now living in New York City, was not happy that TR was away so often on business. On February 13, 1884, while he was in Albany, TR received a telegram with the joyous news that Alice had given birth to a healthy baby girl the previous night.

Only a few hours later, however, another telegram arrived. This one told him that his mother was very ill, and that his young wife's life was also in danger. Mittie had typhoid fever, and Alice had Bright's disease—an infection that causes the kidneys to fail. "There is a curse on this house," said TR's brother Elliott. "Mother is dying, and Alice is dying, too."

Mittie passed away in the early morning hours of February 14, and Alice died in TR's arms later that same day. Beneath a large black X in his diary, on Valentine's Day, he wrote: "The light has gone out of my life."

On a single day in 1884, Theodore Roosevelt's life had been shattered. His mother was dead, his wife was dead, and his newborn daughter was now motherless. "It was a grim and evil fate," he wrote one month later, "but I never have believed it did any good to flinch or yield to any blow, nor does it lighten the blow to cease from working."

His first task was to provide for his daughter, who was named Alice Lee in honor of her mother. The job of caring for baby Alice fell to TR's older sister, Bamie. In March 1884, TR signed a contract for the construction of a house in Oyster Bay, on the north shore of Long Island, New York. While his wife was alive he had planned to call the house Leeholm. Later, the Oyster Bay mansion was named Sagamore Hill. It would become TR's retreat from the cares of the world, and it was known as the "summer White House" while he was president.

J 88.266

RANCHING IN DAKOTA

Never one to shirk his duties, TR finished up his work in the New York State assembly during the spring of 1884. Next he turned westward—first to Utica, New York, for the state Republican convention, and then, a month later, to Chicago, Illinois, where the national Republican convention was held to nominate a candidate for president. After the Chicago convention, TR could have returned to New York and run for another term in the assembly. TR's grief was too deep, however,

This 1884 cartoon by Thomas Nast depicts Roosevelt (left) working together with New York governor Grover Cleveland to reform politics in the state.

TR spent some of the happiest days of his life riding, ranching, and hunting in the Badlands of the Dakota Territory.

Each of TR's two cattle ranches had its own distinctive brand. The Chimney Butte Ranch's cross-shaped brand became so familiar that the property was later known as the Maltese Cross Ranch.

CHIMNEY BUTTE RANCH.
THEODORE ROOSEVELT, Proprietor.
FERRIS & MERRIFIELD, Managers.

P. O. address,
Little Missouri,
D. T. Range,
Little Missouri,
8 miles south
of railroad.

as in cut
on left
hip and
right
side, both or
either, and
own cut dewlap.
Horse brand, on left hip.

ELKHORN RANCH.
THEODORE ROOSEVELT, Proprietor.
SEAWALL & DOW, Managers.

P. O. address, Lit-
le Missouri, D. T.
Range, Little Mis-
souri, twenty-five
miles north of rail-
road.

as in cut, on
left side,
on right,
or the re-
verse.
Horse brand,
on right or
left should-
er.

CONCORD CATTLE COMPANY.

and he was tired of breathing the stale air of New York politics. "I am going cattle-ranching in Dakota for the remainder of the summer and part of the fall," he told a reporter. "What I shall do after that I cannot tell you."

This journey was not the first time TR had been out to the Dakota Territory. A year earlier, he had taken a hunting trip to the Badlands, a region he described as "a land of vast silent spaces, a place of grim beauty." In this region, the basin of the Little Missouri River, in what is now the southwestern corner of North Dakota, was excellent grass-growing country. Land was cheap here, and like many other people in the early 1880s, TR thought he could make a profit by investing in the cattle business. He put money into two cattle ranches, the Maltese Cross and the Elkhorn, and he worked the land for month after month as a rancher, rider, and hunter.

Harsh weather and hard times soon put an end to the ranching boom, but TR had a wonderful time while it lasted. The rugged climate and rough work made him much stronger and healthier. William Sewall, one of the men who came with him to the Badlands, wrote that when TR left the ranching business, he "was as husky as almost any man I have ever seen who wasn't dependent on his arms for a livelihood. He weighed one hundred and fifty pounds and was clear bone, muscle, and grit."

TR Beats a Bully

One famous story about Roosevelt's Dakota days concerns an evening when he beat up a drunken bully in a barroom brawl. When the bully caught a glimpse of TR—who, as usual, was wearing spectacles—he loudly announced that "Four-Eyes" was going to buy drinks for everyone in the bar. The tale continues in TR's own words:

He started leaning over me, a gun in each hand, using very foul language. … In response to his reiterated [repeated] command that I should set up the drinks, I said, "Well, if I've got to, I've got to," and rose, looking past him. As I rose, I struck quick and hard with my right just to one side of the point of his jaw, hitting with my left as I straightened out, and then again with my right. He fired the guns, but I do not know whether this was merely a convulsive action of his hands, or whether he was trying to shoot at me. When he went down he struck the corner of the bar with his head.

As U.S. president, TR revisited the region where he had rebuilt his life two decades earlier. In this photo, TR and his companions ride at full gallop across an Idaho plain.

During the autumn of 1885, while on a visit back home in New York, Roosevelt bumped into an old friend—Edith Carow. There is little evidence that TR fell head over heels in love with her, as he had with his first wife Alice. But Edith was an attractive and intelligent woman, with a thirst for books that was as strong as TR's own. She also knew her own heart, as this letter of June 1886 makes clear:

TR's second wife, Edith Kermit Carow Roosevelt, circa 1900.

TR in 1903 with Edith and their six children (left to right): Quentin, Ted, Archie, Alice, Kermit, and Ethel.

You may not believe it, but I never used to think much about my looks if I knew my dress was all right; now I do care about being pretty for you, and every girl I see I think, "I wonder if I am as pretty as she is," or "At any rate I am not quite as ugly as that girl." ...You know I love you very much and would do anything in the world to please you. ... You know all about me darling. I never could have loved anyone else. I love you with all the passion of a girl who has never loved before. ...

TR and Edith were married later that year, on a foggy December day in London, England. During the next eleven years, she gave birth to four sons and a daughter. She was an excellent household manager and a fine mother, not only to her own children but to TR's first child, Alice.

With a growing family to support, Roosevelt abandoned the risky ranching business and returned to writing, politics, and public service. Just before he married Edith, he had run for mayor

of New York City, but he finished a poor third. Between 1886 and 1889 he published a half dozen books, including the first two parts of his four-volume history series, *The Winning of the West.*

During the autumn of 1888, Roosevelt took time off from his writing to campaign for the Republican presidential nominee, Benjamin Harrison. When Harrison won, TR hoped to be named assistant secretary of state, but the job went to someone else. In the spring of 1889, however, TR was summoned to Washington to become one of three members of the Civil Service Commission.

For anyone but TR, this position might have been a dead-end job. In theory, the Civil Service Commission was supposed to make sure that the people who worked for the government were chosen on merit and not just because of their party loyalty. In reality, however, the commission had little power, and many people who were picked for government jobs were nothing but party hacks. The practice of giving out government jobs as a reward to party loyalists, whether qualified or not, was known as the **spoils system**.

TR believed that government could do good, but only if it was staffed by good people. He used the law—and the power of publicity—to get rid of unqualified and dishonest employees, whether they were Democrats or Republicans. By crusading against the spoils system, he made enemies within his own party. But he proved that even a minor office could be a major platform for change, if a reformer had a message that people wanted to hear.

TR as an Author

During his lifetime, Theodore Roosevelt wrote about three dozen books. Most of them are still in print. Not surprisingly, politics and history were two of TR's favorite subjects. In addition to *The Winning of the West,* TR wrote well-known histories of New York and of the battle between the U.S. and British navies during the War of 1812. He also wrote many books about his life, including his hunting trips and other travels.

CHAPTER 5

ROUGH RIDER

In the 1890s, Roosevelt reformed New York City's police force by getting rid of corrupt, incompetent, and brutal cops.

After six years in Washington, Roosevelt returned with his family to New York City in 1895. A reform-minded businessman, William Strong, had just been elected mayor, and he wanted TR to become commissioner of police. New York City was notorious for its political corruption, and no part of government was more corrupt than the police department. TR liked to tell a story about one job seeker who insisted the police force had to hire him. Why should he be offered a police job? Because, said the applicant, he was too much of a drunkard to do anything else!

As head of the police board, TR took his job seriously. He got rid of corrupt and brutal officials, and he became famous for walking the city streets after midnight, searching for policemen who were goofing off or otherwise misbehaving. The commissioner's exploits were front-page news throughout the city. "Policemen Didn't Dream the President of the Board Was Catching Them Napping," read one newspaper headline.

TR also became an ally of investigative reporters such as Jacob Riis and Lincoln Steffens. Known as **muckrakers**, these reporters sought to expose wrongdoing by corrupt politicians and greedy companies.

Even as he toiled to clean up New York City's police department, Roosevelt had his eye on developments in the nation's capital, as well as throughout the world. President Grover Cleveland, a Democrat, decided not to run for reelection in 1896, so that year's presidential race was thrown wide open. The Republicans chose William McKinley, the former governor of Ohio, while the Democrats nominated William Jennings Bryan. Bryan was renowned for his brilliant, fiery speeches. McKinley, on the other hand, was a dull speaker. The Republican Party spent millions of dollars on McKinley's campaign, however, and Roosevelt made many speeches on his behalf. When McKinley won, TR—not yet forty years old—became assistant secretary of the Navy.

This position proved to be an important one for Roosevelt. His boss, Navy secretary John D. Long, was a kindly gentleman but had little interest in actually running the department. When Long was away from his desk—which was often—he gave TR a free hand. In the late 1890s, before the invention of guided missiles or even airplanes, a nation needed a strong navy to defend its interests overseas. If the United States was going to be a great power, TR believed, it would need to develop a better navy.

Riis and Roosevelt

In his book *How the Other Half Lives* (1890), Jacob Riis exposed the problems faced by poor immigrants in the slums of New York City. Riis was a reporter at the *Evening Sun* newspaper, which is where TR went looking for him. TR left a card for Riis saying he had read the book and wanted to help. "That was all, and it tells the whole story of the man," Riis wrote later. "I loved him from the day I first saw him; nor ever in all the years that have passed has he failed of the promise made then. No one ever helped as he did."

The muckraker Jacob Riis photographed these tailors and other immigrants in New York City who worked long hours in miserable conditions for low pay.

Elelected in 1896, William Mckinley was U.S. president during the Spanish-American War. This photo shows McKinley addressing an audience in 1901, after he won reelection with Roosevelt as his running mate.

If the United States did try to extend its influence, however, it risked conflict with other countries. TR did not think such conflict should be avoided. A war, TR believed, would give the United States a chance to flex its muscles and begin building an empire. War would also give TR a chance to do something his father had never done—show heroism on the battlefield.

THE SPANISH-AMERICAN WAR

The United States saw an opportunity to expand its power in places where Spain had colonies. In the Pacific Ocean, Spain held the Philippines and several other island groups; in the Caribbean Sea (part of the Atlantic Ocean), Spain controlled Cuba and Puerto Rico. Of all these islands, Cuba, just 90 miles (144 kilometers) south of Florida, was closest to the United States.

The seeds of the Spanish-American War had been sown in 1895, when Cubans revolted against Spanish rule and Spain sent thousands of troops to put down the rebellion. Americans were appalled by the brutality of the Spaniards. Stories about suffering Cubans were eagerly reported by U.S. newspapers, which demanded that President McKinley take action. He dispatched one of the nation's most modern warships, the USS *Maine*, which steamed into the Cuban port of Havana in January 1898.

On February 15, as the *Maine* sat at anchor, a huge explosion tore the ship apart. More than 260 crewmen were killed as the *Maine* sank to the bottom of Havana harbor. In a prime example of **yellow journalism**, U.S. newspapers blamed Spain for the blast on the basis of very slim evidence.

With most newspapers loudly calling for war, TR did not feel the need to wait for proof that Spain had sunk the U.S. vessel. While Navy secretary Long was away, TR gave orders to ready all U.S. warships for battle and placed orders for weapons, coal, and other supplies. "I may not be supported," he told a friend, "but I have done what I know to be right; some day they will understand." He also sent an order to Commodore George Dewey, commander of the U.S. Pacific fleet, that if war was declared, Dewey's ships were to attack the Spanish fleet in the Philippines.

Illustrations such as this one, depicting the explosion of the USS *Maine*, put pressure on President McKinley to take action against Spain in Cuba.

THE CUBA CAMPAIGN

Roosevelt did more than simply sit behind a desk and issue orders. When the United States went to war with Spain, he gave up his Washington job to become a lieutenant-colonel in the cavalry regiment that became known as the Rough Riders. By the end of June, he had been promoted to full colonel and was commander of the regiment.

The Rough Riders were an odd assortment of more than one thousand easterners and westerners—cowboys, Indians, and former college athletes—all chosen for their ability to ride horses and shoot. Somehow, TR was able to mold them into an effective fighting force. On July 1, 1898, while Spanish guns blazed, he led the Rough Riders and other troops in a charge up Cuba's Kettle Hill, near the city of Santiago. After they captured Kettle Hill and the nearby San Juan Heights,

As a cavalry officer, TR led the Rough Riders to victory in 1898.

The Rough Riders after capturing San Juan Heights. TR stands in the center.

Santiago surrendered. Spanish resistance crumbled, and by the end of July the war was over.

TR was not at all shy about letting Americans know what he and his Rough Riders had accomplished. When he returned home to New York later that summer, the city boy—so weak and wheezy as a child—had become America's favorite soldier.

The Battle of Kettle Hill

Roosevelt recounted his wartime experiences in his book *The Rough Riders* (1899). The following passage describes how, riding his horse Little Texas, he led his men up Kettle Hill—part of what TR called his "crowded hour."

By this time we were all in the spirit of the thing and greatly excited by the charge, the men cheering and running forward between shots. . . . As soon as I was in the line I galloped forward a few yards until I saw that the men were well started, and then galloped back to help [David] Goodrich, who was in command of his troop, get his men across the road so as to attack the hill from that side. . . . Wheeling around, I then again galloped toward the hill, passing the shouting, cheering, firing men, and went up the lane, splashing through a small stream; when I got abreast of the ranch buildings on the top of Kettle Hill, I turned and went up the slope. Being on horseback I was, of course, able to get ahead of the men on foot, excepting my orderly, Henry Bardshar, who had run ahead very fast in order to get better shots at the Spaniards, who were now running out of the ranch buildings. . . . Some forty yards from the top I ran into a wire fence and jumped off Little Texas, turning him loose. He had been scraped by a couple of bullets, one of which nicked my elbow. . . .

THE WHITE HOUSE YEARS

CHAPTER 6

Soon after returning home from Cuba, TR, the hero of Kettle Hill and San Juan Heights, was offered the Republican nomination for governor of New York State. He won the election of November 1898 and took office just before the year ended.

Roosevelt accomplished a great deal during his twenty-four months as governor. He cracked down on **sweatshops**—small factories, often no bigger than apartments, where people worked long hours for low pay under terrible conditions. Under his leadership, New York limited the hours that women and children could be forced to work and reduced the workday for state employees to eight hours. In addition, measures to preserve New York State's parks and wildlife were passed.

FROM GOVERNOR TO PRESIDENT

TR also succeeded in pushing through a tax on certain big businesses that had received benefits from the state. The companies were unhappy, and so was U.S. senator Thomas Platt of New York, a top Republican leader. Platt believed Roosevelt's reforms were undermining big-business support for the Republican Party, and he sought a way to ease TR out of the governor's mansion.

Platt's chance came in 1900, when President McKinley was running for reelection. McKinley's vice president, Garret Augustus Hobart, had died in November 1899, and McKinley needed a new running mate. Platt predicted—correctly—that having TR on the ticket would help McKinley win a second term.

McKinley's principal supporter, a wealthy business-man and U.S. senator named Mark Hanna, did not trust Roosevelt. When he heard about Platt's scheme, he said, "Don't any of you realize that there's only one life between that madman and the presidency?" Since the office of vice president was so weak, Platt was sure TR would have little impact in Washington. Not long after Roosevelt became vice president, however, Platt was proven wrong.

On September 6, 1901, while visiting Buffalo, New York, President McKinley was shot twice in the stomach by Leon Czolgosz, a factory worker and **anarchist**. McKinley lingered for eight days, but doctors could not save him. On September 14, McKinley died. Roosevelt was now the twenty-sixth president of the United States and the youngest president in U.S. history.

This 1905 painting by T. Dart Walker depicts the fatal shooting of President McKinley, which made Theodore Roosevelt the twenty-sixth president of the United States in 1901.

TRUSTBUSTER AND CONSERVATIONIST

Roosevelt became president at a time of great social and economic change. U.S. industries were booming, but a large number of Americans lived in extreme poverty. Muckrakers exposed the hardships that workers had to endure, while **Progressives** called on government to take a more active role in protecting both workers and consumers. Roosevelt sympathized with the Progressives, but he also had to deal with the leaders of his own party, who prided themselves on being friendly to business.

As president, Roosevelt earned a reputation as a **trustbuster** by taking action against railroad, coal, beef, and sugar firms that had grown too big and were treating workers, consumers, and smaller companies unfairly. His goal, he said, was "to see to it that every man has a square deal, no more and no less." Roosevelt did not want to break up most large companies, but he did want to make sure the federal government kept a close watch on how these companies behaved.

In 1906, the muckraker Upton Sinclair published a novel, *The Jungle*, that exposed the unsanitary conditions in Chicago's stockyards and slaughterhouses. TR responded by getting Congress to pass laws providing for the purity and safety of the nation's foods and medicines.

Nowhere did Roosevelt make a larger mark than as a **conservationist**. He understood that the country's great natural treasures—its forests, rivers, lakes, and wildlife—needed protection, so that

As U.S. president, TR tried to stop powerful railroad companies from charging unfairly high rates to farmers and small businesses.

The title page for *The Jungle* (1906), Upton Sinclair's muckraking look at the meat industry in Chicago.

Slaughterhouses of Chicago

In his novel *The Jungle* (1906), Upton Sinclair provided this unforgettable description of what it felt like to work in Chicago's meat industry during the hottest part of the summer.

All day long the rivers of hot blood poured forth, until, with the sun beating down, and the air motionless, the stench was enough to knock a man over; all the old smells of a generation would be drawn out by this heat—for there was never any washing of the walls and rafters and pillars, and they were caked with the filth of a lifetime. The men who worked on the killing beds would come to reek with foulness, so that you could smell one of them fifty feet away.

In 1903, TR traveled to California to explore Yosemite National Park with conservationist John Muir (right). "I want to drop politics absolutely for four days," he told Muir, "and just be out in the open with you."

future Americans would be able to enjoy them. He established 150 national forests, more than 50 bird reserves, and 4 national game preserves. Through his efforts, the United States government became the protector of about 360,000 square miles (932,400 square kilometers) of forests and other lands. This protected land was equal in size to the combined areas of the states of New York, Virginia, and Tennessee.

TR helped to focus public interest on the presidency. Besides giving the White House its current name, he expanded it to serve the needs of his large family and staff

A "teddy bear" craze began during the presidency of Teddy Roosevelt.

TR and the Teddy Bear

Although Roosevelt won fame as a conservationist and had a genuine love for nature, hunting was his favorite pastime. An unsuccessful hunting trip in 1902 is the source of one of the best known stories about him. Day after day, his companions stalked the woods, looking for something the great man could shoot. Finally, after days of futility, they found a puny bear in the woods. Much to their surprise, TR refused to shoot it.

Reporters picked up the story, saying that TR's refusal to kill the bear showed what a good "sportsman" he was. Much less well known is the fact that the bear had already been mauled by dogs. After TR decided that someone should put the bear "out of its misery," it was killed with a hunting knife.

A cartoon portraying a simplified version of the story became very popular, and toymakers decided to cash in by producing little stuffed bears, which they called "Teddy's bears." The name "teddy bear" stuck and is still used today.

and made it an exciting place in which to live and work. Using his bully pulpit to the fullest, he established a White House press room, making it easier for writers to report everything the president did and said.

CARRYING A BIG STICK

The expression most often credited to Theodore Roosevelt is "Speak softly and carry a big stick." For TR, that "big stick" was the U.S. Navy. A strong navy, however, involved more than just building additional battleships. If the United States was going to expand its military and economic power in both the Atlantic and Pacific Oceans, its navy needed a better way of traveling between the two bodies of water. The most direct route lay through a narrow strip of land that separated them, the **isthmus** of Panama.

When Roosevelt became president in 1901, Panama was a province of Colombia. The governments of the United States and Colombia reached an agreement in 1902 that would have allowed the United States to build and operate a ship canal across the isthmus of Panama. Soon, however, Colombia had second thoughts about the deal. Angry and impatient, TR encouraged a rebel group to take over Panama in 1903.

Political cartoonists often showed TR brandishing a "big stick" in both foreign and domestic policy.

He also sent gunboats to both coasts of Panama to prevent Colombia from putting down the revolt. The United States then quickly signed an agreement with Panama's new leaders.

The 1903 deal gave the United States the right to build a canal and to control the zone on either side of it. In return, Panama received an immediate payment of $10 million and the promise of more money beginning in 1913. Many Americans approved of what Roosevelt had done, but some U.S. senators thought TR had acted improperly. He made no apologies. "I took the canal zone," TR said, "and let Congress debate."

In 1904, Roosevelt was reelected to a full four-year term as president. Two years later, he became the first sitting president to travel outside the United States when he and his wife Edith took a trip to Panama to get a firsthand look at the construction of the canal. Completed in 1914 at a cost of more than $300 million, the Panama Canal remains one of TR's lasting legacies.

Completed in 1914, the Panama Canal provided a direct path between the Pacific and Atlantic Oceans, by way of the Gulf of Panama and the Caribbean Sea.

CARIBBEAN SEA

COSTA RICA

PANAMA CANAL

N

PANAMA

NORTH PACIFIC OCEAN

GULF OF PANAMA

COLOMBIA

The Panama Canal Today

For many decades, the United States managed the Panama Canal, and the U.S. flag flew over the canal zone. During that time, however, resentment grew in Panama about the 1903 agreement and the way it had been reached.

In 1977, the governments of the United States and Panama decided to scrap the 1903 treaty. The United States gave up the canal zone and agreed to let Panama take over the running of the canal at the end of 1999. Today, although a Panama government agency operates the canal, the United States retains the right for its warships to pass through the canal at any time.

When Roosevelt's second term ended in March 1909, he might have retired to the ease and comfort of his Sagamore Hill home. Instead, he launched into his post-presidential career with the same restless energy he'd brought to all his other endeavors. TR went on a hunting safari in Africa, collecting many specimens for the Smithsonian museum in Washington, D.C. He toured the major capitals of Europe. He gave speeches, wrote books, published articles, and even served as a magazine editor. He showed every sign that he enjoyed retirement—but not as much as he had enjoyed being president.

After leaving the White House in 1909, TR went on safari in Africa with his son Kermit.

Honoring TR

While touring Europe in 1910, Roosevelt stopped in Oslo, Norway, to accept a high honor—the Nobel Peace Prize. TR had been awarded the prize four years earlier for helping end the Russo-Japanese War of 1904–1905. Some of the peace talks between Russia and Japan took place at TR's Sagamore Hill home. The prize included a gold medal and a large amount of cash. TR gave the money to charity.

One of the highest awards any American can receive is the Medal of Honor. This award is given to soldiers who show uncommon valor in battle, as TR did in Cuba in 1898. For reasons that remain unclear, TR was passed over for this honor during his lifetime. For decades, his admirers worked to get the mistake corrected. He was finally granted the award in 2001, eighty-two years after his death. Both the Nobel gold medal and the Medal of Honor are now displayed in the Roosevelt Room of the White House.

As the 1912 candidate for the Progressive, or "Bull Moose," Party, TR—shown wearing moose antlers in this cartoon—attempted to appeal to all regions of the country. His acceptance of the "lily white" bouquet of flowers refers to his party's softened stance on equal rights for Southern blacks, in order to attract the votes of white Southerners.

After TR left the presidency, several opposing factions emerged in the Republican Party. One faction was led by the man who had followed Roosevelt into the White House—William Howard Taft. Taft had run for president in 1908 with Roosevelt's blessing. But Taft lacked TR's genius for handling the press and did not share his zeal for reform.

Progressives in the party turned to Roosevelt, and he was ready to heed their call. In early 1912 he agreed to challenge Taft for the Republican presidential nomination. TR was still very popular, but Taft had the support of Republican leaders, who favored Taft's go-slow approach. When Taft became the Republican nominee, TR felt he had no choice but to leave the party. He and other reform-minded Republicans joined forces under the banner of the Progressive, or "Bull Moose," Party.

The Progressives had a remarkably forward-looking platform. They proposed new programs to help the ill, the elderly, and the unemployed, and they supported full voting rights for women. Many of their reforms eventually became law.

TR did not win the 1912 election, but he had the satisfaction of gaining more votes than Taft, who carried only two states, Vermont and Utah. The winner by a wide margin was a moderate reformer, Woodrow Wilson, the Democratic governor of New Jersey.

It Takes More Than a Bullet

Roosevelt was preparing to give a campaign speech in Milwaukee, Wisconsin, on October 14, 1912, when he was shot in the chest. As the bullet passed through his coat, it was slowed by the folded text of his speech and by the case he used for his spectacles. Although the wound was painful, it was not life-threatening, and TR refused to go to the hospital. Instead, he addressed the crowd as planned. "Friends," he began, "I shall ask you to be as quiet as possible. I don't know whether you fully understand that I have just been shot; but it takes more than that to kill a Bull Moose."

THE FINAL YEARS

Roosevelt remained a popular figure after 1912, but he was never again a candidate for public office. He turned down offers to run for president on the Progressive ticket in 1916 and to run for New York State governor as a Republican two years later. He continued to give speeches and write books and articles, however, so the public never doubted where he stood on the leading questions of the day.

In February 1914, with support from the Brazilian government and the American Museum of Natural History, TR explored Brazil's Rio da Dúvida, or River of Doubt—later renamed the Rio Roosevelt or Rio Teodoro in his honor. During the journey his leg became infected, and for forty-eight hours he was crazed with fever. Later, when asked why he had risked the journey, he replied, "I had to go. It was my last chance to be a boy."

When the United States entered **World War I** in 1917, TR was too old to fight, but all four of his sons signed up, and his daughter Ethel served with the Red

TR almost died while exploring Brazil's River of Doubt in 1914. "The Brazilian wilderness stole away 10 years of my life," he wrote to a friend.

Cross. The true cost of war was brought home to him in July 1918, when he and Edith learned that their youngest son, Quentin, a fighter pilot, had been killed while battling the Germans. "It is very dreadful that he should have been killed," said TR. "It would have been worse if he had not gone." Another son, Archibald ("Archie"), was seriously wounded and was sent back home from France to recover.

By late 1918, when he turned sixty, TR was feeling tired and weak—signs of advancing age and heart disease. His heart gave out while he was asleep in his bed at Sagamore Hill, at about fifteen minutes past four on the morning of January 6, 1919. It was Archie who had the task of letting his brothers in Europe know what had happened. His cable echoed what TR may have felt at his own father's passing forty-one years earlier: "The old lion is dead."

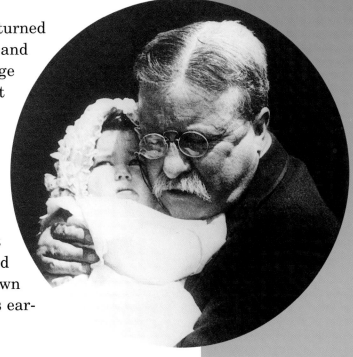

Taken in 1918, not long before his death, this photo of TR shows him cradling his baby granddaughter, Edith Roosevelt Derby. The baby's mother, TR's daughter Ethel, was married at Sagamore Hill in 1913.

Sagamore Hill

Sagamore Hill, Theodore Roosevelt's mansion in Oyster Bay, New York, takes its name from *sagamore*, an Indian word for "chief." TR lived with his family at Sagamore Hill for many years, and his wife Edith continued to live there after his death in 1919. Today, the home is maintained as a historic site by the National Park Service. Furnished just as it was during TR's lifetime, the house is filled with the animal tusks, heads, horns, and skins he brought back from his travels. The house also holds an impressive book collection—about six thousand volumes in all. A visit to Sagamore Hill usually takes about two hours.

1858	Theodore Roosevelt is born October 27, in New York City.
1876	Enters Harvard College.
1878	TR's father dies February 9.
1880	TR graduates from Harvard College. Joins the Republican Party. Marries Alice Hathaway Lee.
1881	Wins a seat in the New York State assembly.
1884	TR's wife and mother die February 14, two days after the birth of his first child. He becomes a rancher in the Dakota Territory.
1886	Marries Edith Kermit Carow; between 1887 and 1897 they have five children together.
1889	Joins the Civil Service Commission in Washington, D.C.
1895	Returns to New York City as police commissioner.
1897	Appointed assistant secretary of the U.S. Navy by President William McKinley.
1898	Serves with the 1st Volunteer Cavalry Regiment (the "Rough Riders") in Cuba during the Spanish-American War. Elected governor of New York State.
1900	Wins election as President McKinley's vice president.
1901	President McKinley is shot September 6; eight days later, upon McKinley's death, TR becomes U.S. president.
1903	Treaty with Panama provides for construction of the Panama Canal (completed in 1914).
1904	TR reelected as president.
1906	Wins Nobel Peace Prize.
1909	Tours Africa and Europe after leaving the presidency.
1912	Runs for president as a Progressive but loses to Democratic candidate Woodrow Wilson.
1919	Dies January 6 at his home in Oyster Bay, New York.

anarchist: someone who opposes all government authority.

bully pulpit: a term coined by TR to describe his use of the U.S. presidency to influence public opinion.

cavalry regiment: a group of soldiers who fought on horseback.

Civil War: in U.S. history, the conflict (1861–1865) between the Union (Northern states) and the Confederacy (Southern states). Slavery in Southern states was a major cause of the conflict, which was won by the Union.

Confederacy: the group of southern states that withdrew from the Union in 1860 and 1861.

conservationist: a person who seeks to preserve, protect, or restore the natural environment.

isthmus: a narrow strip of land linking two larger land masses.

muckrakers: writers who expose wrongdoing by politicians and companies.

Progressives: members of a U.S. political movement that favored large-scale social and economic reforms.

Spanish-American War: a conflict between the United States and Spain in 1898. Upon losing the war, Spain gave up control of Cuba, Puerto Rico, and the Philippine Islands.

spoils system: the awarding of government jobs to a winning party's most loyal supporters, regardless of the qualifications of those supporters.

sweatshops: factories where people work long hours for low pay under terrible conditions.

taxidermy: the art of preparing, stuffing, and mounting dead animals so the creatures look lifelike.

trustbuster: someone who enforces laws that prevent big companies from taking unfair advantage of employees, consumers, and smaller companies.

World War I: a conflict (1914–1918) fought mainly in Europe. The United States entered the war in 1917, siding with England and France against Germany and Austria-Hungary.

yellow journalism: newspaper reporting that wildly exaggerates or distorts the truth.

BOOKS

Fritz, Jean. *Bully for You, Teddy Roosevelt!* New York: Putnam, 1991.

McCullough, David. *Mornings on Horseback.* New York: Simon & Schuster, 2001 (orig. 1981).

Parks, Edd Winfield. *Teddy Roosevelt: Young Rough Rider.* New York: Aladdin Books, 1989.

Roosevelt, Theodore. *The Boyhood Diary of Theodore Roosevelt, 1869–1870.* Mankato, Minn.: Blue Earth Books, 2001.

Schuman, Michael A. *Theodore Roosevelt.* Springfield, N.J.: Enslow, 1997.

INTERNET SITES

American Experience: Mount Rushmore
http://www.pbs.org/wgbh/amex/rushmore/
A PBS web site that spotlights the famous U.S. monument.

Panama Canal
http://www.pancanal.com/eng/index.html
Official site of the Panama Canal Authority.

Presidents of the United States
http://www.whitehouse.gov/history/presidents/
A web site with profiles of all the U.S. presidents, including Theodore Roosevelt.

Theodore Roosevelt Association
http://www.theodoreroosevelt.org/
The web site for a group that seeks to keep alive the memory of TR's life and works.

Theodore Roosevelt: His Life and Times on Film
http://memory.loc.gov/ammem/trfhtml/trfhome.html
Film and sound clips about Theodore Roosevelt from the Library of Congress.

Theodore Roosevelt: Icon of the American Century
http://www.npg.si.edu/exh/roosevelt/
Photos and portraits of Theodore Roosevelt and other important Americans.

INDEX

INDEX *(continued)*

About the Author

Geoffrey M. Horn is a freelance writer and editor with a lifelong interest in politics and the arts. He is the author of books for young people and adults, and has contributed hundreds of articles to encyclopedias and other reference books, including *The World Almanac*. He graduated summa cum laude with a bachelor's degree in English literature from Columbia University, in New York City, and holds a master's degree with honors from St. John's College, Cambridge, England. He lives in southwestern Virginia, in the foothills of the Blue Ridge Mountains, with his wife, four cats (at last count), and one rambunctious collie. This book is dedicated to Lisa and Zeev.